WHO LET THE FROGS OUT?

Don't miss any of the cases in the Hardy Boys Clue Book series!

HARDY BOYS

➤ Clue Book ➤

#9

WHO LET THE FROGS OUT?

BY FRANKLIN W. DIXON ⬌ ILLUSTRATED BY SANTY GUTIÉRREZ

ALADDIN

NEW YORK   LONDON   TORONTO   SYDNEY   NEW DELHI

This book is a work of fiction. Any references to historical events, real people, or real places are used fictitiously. Other names, characters, places, and events are products of the author's imagination, and any resemblance to actual events or places or persons, living or dead, is entirely coincidental.

ALADDIN

An imprint of Simon & Schuster Children's Publishing Division
1230 Avenue of the Americas, New York, NY 10020
First Aladdin paperback edition April 2019
Text copyright © 2019 by Simon & Schuster, Inc.
Illustrations copyright © 2019 by Santy Gutiérrez

For information about special discounts for bulk purchases, please contact
Simon & Schuster Special Sales at 1-866-506-1949 or business@simonandschuster.com.
The Simon & Schuster Speakers Bureau can bring authors to your live event.
For more information or to book an event contact the Simon & Schuster Speakers Bureau
at 1-866-248-3049 or visit our website at www.simonspeakers.com.
Series designed by Karina Granda
Cover designed by Nina Simoneaux
The text of this book was set in Adobe Garamond Pro.
Manufactured in the United States of America 0319 OFF
2 4 6 8 10 9 7 5 3 1
Library of Congress Cataloging-in-Publication Data
Names: Dixon, Franklin W., author. | Gutiérrez, Santy, 1971- illustrator. | Title: Who let the frogs out? / by Franklin W. Dixon ; illustrated by Santy Gutierrez. | Description: First Aladdin hardcover/paperback edition. | New York : Aladdin, [2019] | Series: Hardy Boys clue book ; #9 | Summary: Detective brothers Frank and Joe work to solve a muddy mystery when the spring break Mud Bud Run is canceled due to a frog infestation.
Identifiers: LCCN 2018011582 (print) | LCCN 2018018256 (eBook) |
ISBN 9781534414877 (eBook) | ISBN 9781534414853 (pbk) | ISBN 9781534414860 (hc)
Subjects: | CYAC: Frogs—Fiction. | Mud—Fiction. | Racing—Fiction. | Brothers—Fiction. | Mystery and detective stories.
Classification: LCC PZ7.D644 (eBook) | LCC PZ7.D644 Who 2019 (print) |
DDC [Fic]—dc23
LC record available at https://lccn.loc.gov/2018011582

CONTENTS

Chapter 1

MUD BUDS

"Is this mud run going to be cool or what, Frank?" eight-year-old Joe Hardy asked his brother. "How often do I get to be dirty from head to toe?"

"Hmm," nine-year-old Frank joked, rubbing his chin thoughtfully. "Every day?"

Their friend Chet Morton chuckled, "Funny, Frank!"

"Yeah," Joe said with a smirk. "Very funny."

It was Monday morning and the first day of spring break. It was also the day before the first annual Mud Bud Run through the muddiest part of Bayport Park.

"Hi, guys," a voice called. "Ready to get muddy?"

The boys turned to see Coach Lambert, a gym teacher at Bayport Elementary School, walking over. He had organized the mud run.

"I'm not sure I want to enter the run, Coach Lambert," Chet admitted. "Unless maybe there's a yummy prize at the end?"

"Yummy?" Coach Lambert asked.

"Like something good to eat!" said Chet with a smile.

"There is no prize, Chet, because it's not a race," Coach Lambert said, smiling too. "Just a chance to get muddy and have fun."

The coach pointed to the sign-up table and said, "But you do get a free T-shirt if you sign up."

"Okay, thanks, Coach," Chet sighed.

"Don't forget, guys," Coach Lambert told the

Hardys and Chet, "the Mud Run kicks off at eleven o'clock sharp tomorrow morning."

The coach turned and walked away. When he was out of earshot, Chet said, "Free T-shirts? Why can't it be free doughnuts or smoothies or chicken tacos?"

Frank and Joe traded grins. Their friend loved to snack more than anything!

"When aren't you thinking about food, Chet?" Joe asked. "When you're asleep?"

"Nope," Chet said with a grin. "That's when I'm dreaming about food!"

Before signing up, Frank, Joe, and Chet checked out the mud pit. In it was a rubber tire wall to climb over, a curly slide, and a long giant tube to crawl through.

"The mud will make everything super slippery!" Joe said excitedly. But not everyone was excited about the Mud Bud Run. . . .

"Hey, what's going on over there?" Chet asked. He pointed to a giant structure made of ski poles and tons of plastic wrap by the mud pit.

Eight-year-old Daisy Zamora and her six-year-old

twin brothers, Matty and Scotty, were busily creating the structure. They had put up a huge sign that read, THE MUCK STOPS HERE! MUDDY BUDDIES ARE FUDDY DUDDIES!

"What's their problem with the Mud Bud Run?" asked Joe.

"And what's with that weird fort they're building?" Frank wondered. "Let's see what's up."

The boys approached the Zamoras. When they asked about the sign and fort, Daisy explained, "This mud run is the worst. It's going to totally ruin our garden. We're putting up all this plastic wrap to try to protect it."

"What garden?" Chet asked.

"Our pizza topping garden!" Scotty replied.

The Zamoras pulled some plastic wrap aside to reveal a circular garden separated into parts—just like a pizza. A different kind of plant was growing in each section.

When it came to pizza, the Zamora kids were practically experts. Their parents owned the Pizza Palace on Bay Street.

"We're growing basil, oregano, tomatoes, peppers," Daisy said. "Even kale."

"Kale?" Chet cried. "If you know so much about pizza, where are my favorite toppings, like pepperoni and extra cheese?"

Matty rolled his eyes. "You don't grow pepperoni and cheese, smarty-pants!" he exclaimed.

"What difference does it make, Matty?" Daisy

sighed. "After tomorrow our garden will be covered with mud and ruined. There's no way this stuff will protect it the whole day."

"That's why we hate the Mud Bud Run!" Matty said.

"Now I get it," Frank admitted. "But why use the community garden right in the middle of a busy park?"

"Shouldn't it be safe in your backyard," asked Joe, "or behind the pizzeria?"

"Not if we want to spread the word about our pizza place," Daisy explained. "If people see all these fresh toppings, they'll head to our pizzeria in swarms!"

"I hate to tell you this," Chet said, pointing to the plants, "but your garden is already swarming— with bugs!"

Huh?? Daisy, Matty, and Scotty glanced down and groaned. Chet was right. Creepy crawlies had invaded their pizza topping garden!

"Oh no!" Daisy cried. "The bugs are back!"

Scotty turned to Matty. "And they call us pests," he said.

Frank, Joe, and Chet headed back toward the mud pit, leaving the Zamoras to deal with the bugs.

"Can we please sign up for the mud run already?" Frank asked.

"Sure, Frank," said Joe. "Nothing can stop us now!"

But halfway to the sign-up table a boy from Frank's grade jumped into their path. He was dressed in dark clothes from head to toe.

With a nod at Frank and Joe, he said, "You guys are the Hardys, right? Those kid detectives from school?"

Joe smiled proudly as he pulled a book from his pocket. "Does this answer your question?" he asked.

"What's that?" the boy asked.

"It's our clue book," Frank said, "where we write down our suspects and clues."

"And answer the five most important questions a detective can ask," Joe explained. "*Who, what, where, when,* and *why.*"

Joe opened the clue book to the five *W*s written on a page. "See what I mean?"

The boy looked at the page and shrugged. "I guess," he said.

"You look familiar," Joe told the boy. "But I can't think of your name."

"I thought everyone knew me," the boy said. "Does the name Oliver Splathall ring a bell?"

"Sure," said Chet. "You're the guy in school who makes all those sculptures."

"Sand sculptures in the summer," Frank said. "Leaf-pile sculptures in the fall."

"Snow sculptures in the winter," Joe went on, "and in the spring—mud pies!"

"They are not mud pies!" Oliver gasped. "They are earth-infused statues combined with the collective sense of the sublime."

Frank, Joe, and Chet all stared at Oliver.

"Anyway . . . I stopped you because I need a detective," Oliver explained, "to find out whose dumb idea it was to have this mud run."

"That's easy," Joe said. "It was Coach Lambert's."

"I knew you would be good, thanks!" Oliver said with a smile. "Now I just have to talk Coach Lambert into calling the whole thing off."

"Calling off the mud run?" Joe asked. "Why?"

"Every spring I use mud from that pit to make my sculptures," Oliver explained. "With so many kids running through, its perfectly lumpy texture will be ruined."

"Perfectly lumpy texture?" Chet murmured to himself. "I thought mud was mud."

"Sorry, Oliver," Frank said. "But I don't think the coach will call the mud run off."

"Most of the kids can't wait for it tomorrow," Joe added.

"And my fans can't wait for my mud sculpture show in two days!" Oliver said before turning away in a huff.

"Where are you going, Ollie?" called Joe.

"To think of another plan," Oliver called back. "And don't call me Ollie!!"

As Oliver walked away, Joe asked, "What do you think his plan will be?"

"All I know is that our plan is to be in this mud run tomorrow," Frank declared. "So let's sign up once and for all!"

The Hardys and Chet walked alongside the mud pit toward the sign-up table. They were almost there when a frantic voice shouted, "Out of our way! Out of our way! Out of our way!"

The boys whirled around to see a man racing straight toward them. A pack of dogs was running in front of him—a pack of all breeds and sizes!

"To the side, boys!" the man yelled. "Now!"

Frank, Joe, and Chet looked around. To one side was a hot dog cart. To the other was—

"The mud pit!" Joe shouted. "Everybody jump!"

Chapter 2

SWAMPY SHOCKER

The charging dogs were only feet away when Frank, Joe, and Chet leaped into the pit with a *SPLASH!*

The pit wasn't deep, but it was deep enough to leave their pants splattered!

"Bleeech!" Chet complained.

The man and his canine crew kept charging until the dogs pounced on a hot dog that rolled off the cart. As the man stopped to get control of the pack, the three boys noticed his T-shirt. It read, THE GOLDEN BONE.

"What's the Golden Bone?" asked Chet, his eyes lighting up. "A new place for barbecue ribs?"

Joe shook his head. "It's a fancy spa for dogs," he explained. "Aunt Trudy started taking in foster dogs and sometimes brings them there for special treatments."

"Like Shi Tzu Shiatsu and Stretch and Fetch," Frank added. "Aunt Trudy says the Golden Bone is a very relaxing place."

The dogs seemed to relax after they'd eaten the frank on the ground. But there was nothing relaxed about the man with them as he argued with Coach Lambert, who had approached him and the dogs.

"What do you mean I can't run with my dogs here?" the man demanded. "I am the owner of the Golden Bone spa!"

"I know you are, Mr. Frederick," Coach Lambert said. "But tomorrow is the day of the mud run, so you can't bring your dogs here while it's going on."

"Mud doesn't bother my dogs," Mr. Frederick insisted.

"How do you know?" asked the coach.

"The Golden Bone has a treatment called Soak and Croak," Mr. Frederick explained. "Dogs relax in a mud bath to the soothing sounds of croaking frogs."

"Frogs?" Chet whispered. "Is he serious?"

"My dogs also run in this spot every morning for their Daily Doggy Dash," Mr. Frederick argued. "They must stick with their wellness routine!"

"The dogs can still dash tomorrow, Mr. Frederick,"

Coach Lambert said, "after the kids complete the Mud Bud Run."

Mr. Frederick bit his lip to keep from arguing more. Clutching the leashes tightly, he began walking his dogs away.

Coach Lambert turned to Frank, Joe, and Chet, still standing in the mud pit. "No jumping in the mud pit until the run tomorrow, guys," he said.

The coach left to oversee a delivery of porta-potties. The three boys trudged out of the pit to inspect their mud-splashed jeans.

"I know what we'll be doing tonight," Joe groaned. "Laundry!"

Chet frowned as he stomped mud from his shoes. "I'm out, you guys," he said. "I don't want to do this mud run tomorrow."

"Why not?" asked Frank.

"Because," Chet said, "the only mud I like is Mississippi mud pie!"

After saying good-bye, Chet left to buy a hot dog. Frank and Joe were disappointed but still determined to do the Mud Bud Run together.

"Let's finally sign up for this run." Frank said. "Before they're out of space!"

"And free T-shirts," said Joe with a smile. "Come on, Frank, let's do this!"

The next day couldn't come quickly enough for Frank and Joe. It was the morning of the Mud Bud Run, and the Hardy brothers were ready to get muddy!

It was ten thirty when Frank and Joe walked into the park with Aunt Trudy.

"Too bad Mom and Dad can't watch us run today," Joe said.

"What am I, chicken liver?" Aunt Trudy joked. "I'll be cheering you guys on since your mom and dad are working today."

With a smile, she added, "Not everyone is on spring break, you know."

Frank and Joe smiled too. They were glad their aunt lived in the apartment above the Hardys' garage. With all the cats and dogs she brought home waiting for adoption, they were never alone!

"Have fun, guys," Aunt Trudy said when they

reached the mud pit. After giving them a thumbs-up sign, she joined the crowd of spectators.

Frank and Joe were directed to the starting point. It was underneath a purple-and-yellow balloon arch about ten feet away from the mud pit, and kids had already begun milling around the area.

It wasn't long before Coach Lambert's voice crackled through an electronic bullhorn: "Will all Mud Buds gather at the starting point under the balloon arch so we can start the run?"

"This is it!" said Joe excitedly.

"Ready, Mud Buds?" the coach declared. "On your mark . . . get set . . . GO!"

"Yay, Frank, Joe!" Aunt Trudy shouted. "Show that mud who's boss!!"

The brothers ran with everyone else toward the mud pit. But when the kids up front reached the pit, they stopped short. Their sudden halt sent those behind them bumping to a stop too!

"What happened?" Frank asked.

Ribbit! Croak!

"And what's that weird noise?" added Joe.

The blurps and croaks seemed to be coming from the mud pit. The brothers squeezed through the crowd to see what was up.

At the edge of the pit, they looked down. Frank couldn't believe his eyes. Neither could Joe.

"Holy guacamole, Frank!" Joe shouted. "This mud is hopping—with frogs!"

CASE IN PLACE

Frank and Joe weren't the only ones surprised by the frogs. Michael Sanders, a boy in Joe's third-grade class, pointed to the creatures and shouted, "Dudes, this is soooo cool!"

"Best. Surprise. Ever!" exclaimed Lynn Russo, from Frank's class.

Coach Lambert rushed over. When he saw the frogs, his jaw dropped.

"Thanks for putting them in there, Coach!" Joe said with a smile. "What could be swampier than frogs?"

The coach shook his head hard. "I did not put frogs in the mud!" he insisted. "They weren't here when we set up the obstacle course yesterday!"

Clem, the park's night watchman, stood nearby. "Those frogs weren't here last night, either," he said. "I would have heard those croaks for sure."

"What about early this morning?" Coach Lambert asked, "Before we all got here for the mud run?"

"The park opened at seven," another park employee said. "I walked past the mud pit and there were no frogs anywhere."

The kids waited impatiently, eager to run. Joe tried counting the frogs, but more kept popping up all through the mud pit. So far he'd counted about two dozen. Cool!

"Can we run now, Coach Lambert?" Joe asked.

"Run?" said the coach. He seemed to think about it until he finally said, "I guess we can restart the run. A few frogs never hurt anyone."

Coach Lambert lifted his whistle to his lips. But just as he was about to blow—

"STOP!!!" a voice boomed.

Frank and Joe recognized the voice. It was—

"Aunt Trudy!" Frank gasped.

The brothers' aunt burst through the crowd. She had gotten hold of Coach Lambert's bullhorn and was still shouting through it: "This mud run must be stopped, Coach. I repeat—STOPPED!"

"Um . . . is there a problem, ma'am?" Coach Lambert asked.

Aunt Trudy lowered the bullhorn. "You bet there is," she said. "If the kids run through the mud, all the poor frogs in there will be in danger."

"But the kids want to run," said the coach. "I'm sure they'll be careful not to step on—"

"We must protect all the creatures of the earth!" Aunt Trudy shouted through the bullhorn again. "Warts and all!"

Frank and Joe traded worried looks. Would Aunt Trudy really stop the Mud Bud Run?

"Coach," Aunt Trudy went on, "do you really

want to be blamed for dozens of trampled froggies? Well . . . do you?"

Coach Lambert's eyes began to water. "I caught a frog once when I was a kid," he said. "A tiny frog I named Larry."

"Well, then do it for Larry," Aunt Trudy said gently.

The coach took the bullhorn from her. He raised it to his lips and shouted, "Attention, all runners! The Mud Bud Run is canceled until further notice!"

Disappointed groans rose from the crowd. As the runners sulked away from the mud pit, Aunt Trudy smiled at Frank and Joe.

"Now that I have saved those creatures, I can save one more," she said. "Mind if I head to the animal shelter? I heard there's a wired-haired terrier named Stan who needs a foster home."

"Sure, Aunt Trudy," said Frank. "Joe and I can grab lunch on Bay Street."

Lynn and Michael stood nearby. They watched as Aunt Trudy hurried away.

"She's your aunt?" Michael asked the brothers.

"Your aunt Trudy just stopped the Mud Bud Run!" Lynn complained.

"No, she didn't," Joe insisted. "It was the frogs, and you know it."

"Whatever," Lynn muttered before she and Michael walked away too.

Frank and Joe turned to look at the frog-filled mud pit. Heads kept popping up, joining the chorus of blurps and croaks.

"How did all those frogs get in there?" Joe wondered

out loud. "And right before the Mud Bud Run too?"

To get answers, the brothers spoke to more park workers, even the owner of the hot dog cart. No one had seen frogs in the mud pit before or had any idea how they got there. But then Frank thought of something.

"Maybe someone put the frogs in the mud," he told Joe, "to keep the Mud Bud Run from happening."

"Who would want to stop the Mud Bud Run?" Joe asked.

The froggy croaks were suddenly drowned out by cheers. The brothers glanced to the side, where they saw Daisy, Scotty, and Matty. The smiling Zamoras stood by their pizza garden and its protective fort, trading high fives!

"I just thought of three kids who would want to stop the Mud Bud Run," Frank said. "Daisy, Matty, and Scotty!"

"And I just thought of a reason for a new case," Joe said. He reached into his pocket and pulled out the clue book. "Good thing I brought this."

"You brought it to the mud run?" cried Frank.

"You bet!" Joe replied with a smile. "Wherever we go, so does our clue book—and my favorite pencil with the spaceship eraser!"

On the way to Bay Street, the brothers talked about the case. Joe had already written the five *W*s on his new case page: *who*, *what*, *where*, *when*, and *why*.

"We already know where it happened," Frank pointed out. "The mud pit in Bayport Park."

"We know what happened too," said Joe. "Last I counted, the mud pit was filled with at least two dozen frogs."

He filled in *where* and *what*, but the question of *when* was not so easy.

"Let's backtrack," Frank suggested. "The Mud Run began at eleven sharp. Most of the runners got to the park between ten and ten thirty, like us."

"One guard said there were no frogs in the pit all night," Joe remembered. "The other guard said there no frogs at seven in the morning after the park opened."

"So if the runners got to the park between ten and ten thirty," Frank said, "then someone could have dumped the frogs between seven and ten."

Joe wrote the timeline under the word *when*. "Now we just have to figure out who did it," he said.

"And why," Frank added.

"I'm pretty sure it was Daisy, Matty, and Scotty," Joe insisted. "They didn't want the run to go on because of their pizza garden. They looked pretty happy when it was called off, too."

"Matty and Scotty were suspects in some of our other cases," Frank said as they turned onto Bay

Street. "Most times they were just guilty of being pests!"

"Pesty enough to maybe score all those frogs," Joe said, "and dump them in the mud pit before the run."

On the following page Joe wrote the word *Suspects*. Underneath, he wrote: *Daisy, Matty, and Scotty Zamora*. When he was done, he glanced up from his clue book.

"Can you think of other suspects, Frank?" he asked. "Come on, dude, throw me a bone!"

Bone? Frank's eyes lit up as he said, "The Golden Bone dog spa and Mr. Frederick!"

"What about him?" Joe asked.

"He was mad that he couldn't run with his dogs until the mud run was over," said Frank. "Maybe he filled the mud pit with frogs to get even."

"Okay. Where would Mr. Frederick get all those frogs?" said Joe.

"Didn't he say he had a class called Soak and Croak?" Frank asked. "Where dogs relax to the sound of croaking frogs?"

"He'd have to have frogs at the Golden Bone to do that," Joe said excitedly.

Joe added Mr. Frederick to their suspect list. As he closed his clue book, he nodded toward the Pizza Palace. "Let's go in there, Frank," he said. "Right now."

"So we can question the Zamoras?" asked Frank.

"So I can get a slice," Joe replied with a grin. "Then we'll question the Zamoras!"

The smell of baking dough and garlic filled their noses as Frank and Joe entered the pizzeria. They joined the line of people waiting to order pies and slices. Mrs. Zamora stood at the cash register, taking orders.

Frank and Joe were about to watch Mr. Zamora flip pizza dough when a tall man wearing overalls marched to the front of the line.

"Hello, Mrs. Zamora!" the man said with a smile. "Have you been topping your pizzas with frog legs lately?"

"Frog legs?" Mrs. Zamora cried. "What makes you think that?"

"I'm Bob from Blurpy Bob's Frog Farm right here in Bayport," the man said. "Your kids bought some frogs from my farm yesterday."

"Yes, they told me," Mrs. Zamora said. "What about them?"

Bob held up a can. "The kids forgot their complimentary can of frog chow!"

Frank and Joe stared speechlessly at Blurpy Bob.

Had he just said Daisy, Matty, and Scotty bought frogs? Yesterday?

Chapter 4

HOPPER WHOPPER

Before Mrs. Zamora could take the can of frog chow, Daisy hurried over.

"I'll take that, thank you," she said quickly. She took the can from Blurpy Bob, then rushed to the back of the restaurant.

Frank and Joe waited quietly while Bob left the pizzeria. As soon as Mrs. Zamora helped the next customer, they whispered excitedly.

"Daisy and her brothers bought frogs from

Blurpy Bob," Joe said. "We heard it with our own ears!"

"We know they didn't want the mud run to go on," said Frank. "So—"

"Ready to order, boys?"

Frank and Joe turned their heads toward Mrs. Zamora.

"We'd like to order slices, Mrs. Zamora," Frank told her. "But first, can we talk to Daisy?"

"About homework," Joe added.

"Homework over spring break?" Mrs. Zamora asked. She shrugged and said, "Daisy is in the back room with the twins. They're rolling garlic knots."

Mr. Zamora kept flipping dough as he joked, "I guess you can say they're on a roll!"

The brothers had no trouble finding the door to the back room. Frank knocked only twice when Daisy called, "Come in."

Joe opened the door. He and Frank walked into the room, where Matty and Scotty were busy rolling strips of dough. Daisy stood behind them, supervising.

"You call that a twist?" she asked Scotty. "Tighter, tighter!"

"Okay, okay," Scotty sighed.

"Bossy pants," Matty complained.

Daisy glanced up at Frank and Joe. "If you want garlic knots with your pizza, you'll have to wait," she said. "They're not baked yet."

"We don't want garlic knots now," Frank said. "We just want to know about the frogs you ordered from Blurpy Bob's."

"And what you did with them," said Joe, raising his eyebrow. "Like maybe fill the mud run pit with them?"

"Frogs in the mud?" Daisy scoffed. "Why would we put our frogs in there?"

"Because you and the twins hated the Mud Bud Run," Frank pointed out. "You said it would ruin your pizza topping garden."

"When the run was called off because of the frogs," Joe went on, "you guys were celebrating like it was the Fourth of July."

All three Zamora kids looked surprised.

"Is that why the run was called off?" asked Matty.

"There were frogs in the mud?" Scotty exclaimed. "Whooooa!"

"You didn't know?" Joe asked.

Daisy shook her head. "The runners were already walking away when we got to the park," she said. "We knew the mud run was called off, but we didn't know why."

"Okay, if you didn't use the frogs for the Mud Bud Run, why did you buy them in the first place?" Frank asked Daisy.

"Because frogs eat bugs!" Daisy said. "You saw how many pests were crawling in our pizza garden yesterday."

"We bought a bunch of hungry frogs from Blurpy Bob," Matty said, "and let one loose in our garden!"

"Did you say you got a bunch of frogs, but let only one loose?" asked Frank.

"Maybe," replied Matty.

"What did you do with the other frogs?" Joe

demanded. "Dump them in the mud pit?"

"None of your beeswax!" Matty snapped as he twisted a garlic knot supertight.

Suddenly—*blurp . . . blurp . . . blurp . . .*

Frank and Joe froze. There was no mistaking that noise. It was—

"Frogs!" Frank yelped.

The brothers followed the croaks to a big cardboard box. On it was a green cartoony frog face next to the words: BLURPY BOB'S FROG FARM.

"I'll bet it's some leftover frogs!" Joe said.

Before the brothers could look inside, Daisy and the twins raced over.

"I told you," Daisy said, "we need frogs to help our garden."

"They already helped your garden," Joe said with a frown, "by calling off the Mud Bud Run."

Joe slid the box closer to look inside. Matty and Scotty took hold of the other side. Soon a tug-of-war broke out between the twins and Joe!

"I just want to look inside!" said Joe, pulling one end of the box.

"We don't want you to!" Scotty said, pulling the other end. "They're our frogs!"

"Guys, stop!" Frank said. "You're going to—"

RIIIIIIPPPP!

All five kids froze as the box tore in half. A plastic tank fell out with a *clunk*, popping the lid off. Daisy shrieked as three big croaking frogs hopped out.

"Now look what you did!" Daisy cried.

Frank and Joe scrambled to catch the frogs, but they were too fast. Croaking all the way, the frogs hopped around the room, then out the open door!

"Uh-oh," Scotty groaned.

The kids ran to look out the door. The three frogs hopped all over the pizzeria, around tables and between customers' legs. Mr. and Mrs. Zamora ran frantically to catch them.

"Don't just stand there!" Daisy told the twins. "Let's help Mom and Dad!"

Daisy, Scotty, and Matty left the back room to join the chaos in the restaurant.

"We'd better get out of here, Frank," said Joe.

"Let's pick up the tank first," Frank sighed. "It's the least we can do."

While Joe lifted the plastic frog tank off the floor, Frank noticed something.

"Look what else fell out of the box," he said, reaching down to pick up a small piece of paper. "It looks like a receipt from Blurpy Bob's Frog Farm."

"How many frogs did they buy?" asked Joe. "A dozen? Two dozen?"

"Uh, dude," Frank said, reading the receipt. "Try four."

Chapter
5

HELLO, OLLIE!

"Four frogs? That's it?" Joe exclaimed. He grabbed the receipt to see for himself. "There were at least two dozen of those hoppers in the mud pit this morning."

"So Daisy and her brothers couldn't have put frogs in there," Frank said.

Joe did the math. Four frogs minus the one in the garden equaled three. And the last three were hopping around the pizzeria.

"Okay," he sighed. "But that leaves us with only one suspect: Mr. Frederick."

Joe placed the receipt on a desk in the back room. A desk calendar was turned to that day's date. On the page, written in red marker, were the words *Dentist: Daisy, Matty, Scotty, 7:30, 8:30, 9:30.*

"Another reason the Zamoras couldn't have filled the mud pit with frogs this morning," Joe said, pointing to the calendar. "They were at the dentist!"

The Pizza Palace had become the Screaming Palace as the Hardys made their way toward the front door. They could see Matty holding one frog and Daisy another. Mr. and Mrs. Zamora tried to catch the last frog, which was hopping across the counter.

"Sorry, Daisy!" Joe called out. "You really did order the frogs to eat the garden bugs."

"And now the frogs are eating our pizzas," Daisy shouted back. "Thanks a lot, Hardys!"

Without a word, the brothers left the Pizza Palace and walked away as fast as they could.

Halfway up the block, Joe stopped to draw a line through the Zamora kids' names. They were no longer suspects.

"Hey, Joe, check out the pup!" Frank said.

Joe looked up from his clue book to see a fluffy white Maltese being walked by its proud owner. The little dog was glamorously coiffed with a sparkly collar around its neck.

"Looks like that dog is getting pampered," Joe pointed out. "Her owner is bring her to the Golden Bone."

The brothers watched as the Maltese was led into the Golden Bone's storefront.

"Hey, wait a minute," Frank said. "Isn't Mr. Frederick one of our suspects?"

"Next on our list," Joe confirmed.

He and Frank checked out the spa window. In it was a schedule propped up on a golden easel. It listed that day's classes and treatments.

"Soak and Croak is later today!" Joe said.

"That's the treatment where dogs relax in a mud bath," Frank added, "to the sounds of croaking frogs."

"Let's check out the frogs in Mr. Frederick's spa," Joe said, "so we can be sure he had enough to dump in the mud run!"

"I wish we could go inside and look for frogs," said Frank. "But without a dog, how could we?"

Joe agreed. If only they had a dog. Wait a minute—maybe they did!

"Frank, isn't Aunt Trudy picking up a new foster dog today?" Joe asked.

"Yeah," Frank said. "A terrier named Stan."

A smile spread across Joe's face. "So maybe," he said, "Stan would like a little pup pampering too!"

In a flash the two brothers were back home. Their mom was still at work at the real estate agency, and their dad was at his private investigation office. But Aunt Trudy was home to introduce them to her new foster dog. She also agreed to a Golden Bone visit for Stan. Score!

"Now, remember, boys," Aunt Trudy said, handing Frank a twenty-dollar bill, "get him the Bow-Wow Blowout or the Yip-Yip Flea Dip—but absolutely no mud bath."

The frisky terrier tugged at his leash, making Frank laugh. "Got it, Aunt Trudy!" he called back.

As they walked away from the house, Joe said, "I told you Aunt Trudy would say yes."

The brothers had a blast walking Stan to Bay Street. But just as they were about to enter the Golden Bone, they saw Oliver Splathall leaving Yum-Yum FroYo with a cup of frozen yogurt.

"Hi, Ollie," Joe said. "What's up?"

Oliver rolled his red and tired eyes. "I told you I hate when people call me Ollie!" he groaned. "Do people call you Joey? Or Frankie?"

"Just our grandmother," Joe said.

Oliver ate a spoonful of yogurt while Frank asked, "Did you figure out what to do about your mud sculpture show?"

Oliver's mouth was too full for him to answer, so Joe said, "Just so you know, you can't use the mud pit in the park anytime soon."

"Sure I can," Oliver insisted. "Wait, what are you talking about?"

Oliver's reaction made Joe wonder what he might be up to. He was about to tell Oliver about the frogs when Stan sniffed at the kid artist's boots. Joe reached down to tug Stan away, and he noticed something that made his eyes widen.

"Tell me about the mud pit another time," Oliver said. "I promised my dad I'd meet him at the supermarket."

As Oliver walked away, Joe turned to Frank.

"He wasn't wearing muddy boots yesterday," Joe whispered. "They were super-shiny clean!"

"So?" Frank said with a shrug. "What's the big deal?"

"The big deal is," said Joe, narrowing his eyes, "today his boots are caked with mud!"

SOIL TREATMENT

Frank didn't think the muddy boots were important. "Oliver's a mud sculptor, Joe," he said. "Getting muddy is part of the job."

"Yeah, but did you notice the rest of his clothes?" asked Joe. "Clean as a whistle."

"So?" Frank replied.

"So if he was mud-sculpting, his clothes would be muddy too," Joe explained. "But . . . if he was just filling a muddy field with frogs—"

"Okay, I get it," Frank interrupted. "We can add his name to the suspect list. But if we're going to look for frogs at the Golden Bone, we'd better get hopping!"

Joe chuckled. "Hopping?" he asked. "Was that a corny joke?" He wrote down Oliver's name in their clue book as they walked.

He held the heavy golden door open as Frank led Stan inside the spa. The posh-looking lobby had wall-to-wall white carpeting and portraits of sleek and fluffy dogs on the walls.

A woman dressed in a crisp white pantsuit sat behind a glass reception desk. The nameplate on her desk read SOPHIE.

When Sophie saw Stan, she pulled a dog biscuit from a crystal bowl and held it out. "Bone appétit!" she said with a smile. "Is your dog here for Soak and Croak?"

"Yes!" Joe blurted a bit too eagerly. From the corner of his eye he could see Frank staring at him.

The receptionist pointed down a nearby hall. "Then you'd better hurry. The class started ten minutes ago."

Stan was still crunching on the biscuit as the brothers led him down the hall.

"Are we really bringing Stan to Soak and Croak?" Frank whispered. "You know we promised Aunt Trudy no mud bath."

"It's just a way to get us inside so we can look for frogs," Joe whispered back, "But where do we start?"

The brothers stopped in their tracks when they heard the sound of croaking frogs. It seemed to be coming from behind one of the closed doors.

"Let's start here," Frank said, pointing to the door.

Frank, Joe, and Stan walked through the door into a small room. They could hear frogs but couldn't see any. They did see a window overlooking a pool filled with muddy brown water.

"Whoa!" said Frank, gazing through the window.

Seven dogs were paddling in the pool below. They seemed relaxed as they drifted to the soothing sound of croaking frogs. Perched in a yoga position on the side of the pool was Mr. Frederick, his eyes closed.

Frank dropped Stan's leash so he could jump up

on the window to look too. "I hear frogs," he said. "But where are they?"

"Check it out, Frank," Joe whispered.

Frank turned to see Joe at a nearby table. On it was sleek electronic device the size of a microwave oven. Flashing on the gadget was the word FROGS!

"That looks like a multi-room sound system!" Frank said, walking over to it. "We saw one in

Gadgets Galore when dad was shopping for a car vac, remember?"

"I guess it means Mr. Frederick doesn't use real frogs," Joe said. "Unless he recorded real frogs to get their croaks."

He looked around the room and continued. "Which means there could still be frogs in the house!"

Suddenly—

"Woof!" Stan barked.

Before Frank could grab the dog's leash, he jumped up and put his paws on the table. They landed on the sound system, flipping the switch from softly croaking frogs to loudly meowing cats!

"Turn it back, Joe!" cried Frank, tugging Stan away from the table. "Turn the sound back to frogs!"

Joe flipped the switch, only to get the sound of stampeding elephants!

"Oh nooooo!" he groaned.

"Joe, look!" Frank called.

Joe raced to his brother back at the window. He looked down to see dogs jumping out of the mud

bath. The bathing bowwows were going wild to the sound of elephants, shaking mud off their fur and all over Mr. Frederick!

"All we wanted to do was find frogs!" Frank groaned.

"Yeah," Joe sighed. "Instead we found trouble!"

Chapter

7

TANKS FOR THE CLUE

Joe looked for any way to turn off the sound but had no luck. "I can't find the off switch!" he cried. "Where's the off switch on this thing?"

Frank was still watching the mud-bath commotion from the window. Sophie had run into the mud-bath room to help calm the dogs. She shrieked as her white pantsuit became a muddy mess!

"I don't see Mr. Frederick down there," Frank reported. "Where do you think he went?"

BOOM! Both brothers jumped as the door slammed open. They turned to see a mud-splattered Mr. Frederick. Stan growled softly as the dog spa owner stood fuming in the doorway.

"Uh . . . hi," Frank said, forcing a smile.

"I was just . . . looking for the off switch," said Joe.

Leaving the door open, Mr. Fredrick stomped over to the sound system. He lifted a rubber flap on the side to reveal more buttons. With the tap of a red button, the elephant sounds stopped.

"So that's where it was!" Joe said, smiling. "Did you get that at Gadgets Galore?"

Mr. Frederick didn't answer Joe's question. Instead he asked his own: "Did you boys just switch croaking frogs to howling cats? And then elephants?"

"Yes," Frank admitted, "but we were—"

"You know what happens when dogs hear cats?" Mr. Frederick cut in with wide eyes.

"The fur flies?" Joe joked.

Mr. Frederick wasn't laughing. "It's going to take hours to calm those dogs down," he complained. "They'll never be ready for Dalmatian Lavation!"

"Dalmatian . . . Lavation?" Frank repeated.

"The next bath to wash the mud off," Mr. Frederick explained. He looked down at his muddy clothes and muttered, "I suppose I should be joining them."

"Sorry we ruined your class, Mr. Frederick," Frank said. "We were looking to see where the croaks came from."

"We thought there were real frogs in this room," Joe explained. "Frogs were found at the Mud Bud Run this morning, and we were wondering if maybe they came from here."

"I heard about those frogs," Mr. Frederick said. "But why are you trying to find out where they came from?"

"We're detectives," explained Frank. "We think someone put the frogs in the mud pit."

"And we're trying to find out who!" Joe added.

"So you thought that 'who' . . . was me?" Mr. Frederick asked.

When the brothers didn't answer, Mr. Frederick pointed to the sound system. "As you see, I do not use real frogs," he said. "Just canned croaks all the way."

"We know that now," Frank said, "but you were pretty mad about the mud run yesterday in the park."

"Coach Lambert said you couldn't have the Doggy Dash until the mud run was over," Joe added. "That would have been your *why* for dumping the frogs in the mud."

Mr. Frederick took a deep breath, then said, "I was mad about the mud run, yes. But now I'm very grateful for it."

"Grateful?" Frank and Joe asked together.

"The Mud Bud Run gave me the most fabulous idea last night," Mr. Frederick said. He opened a desk drawer, pulled out a big sheet of paper, and held it up for the boys to see.

Frank and Joe looked at Mr. Frederick's sketch. It was a picture of a park with trees and a little bench. But the interesting stuff was in the center. There was a giant sneaker, a bone, and a tennis ball. Dogs of different sizes were running between them.

"Is that a mud run for dogs?" Joe guessed.

"Correct, young man!" Mr. Frederick declared. "Introducing the Golden Bone's own Muckety-Mutt Meander!"

"Awesome," Frank said.

"Where are you going to build it?" asked Joe.

"Hopefully we can buy the empty lot down the street," Mr. Frederick said.

"It's a great idea," Joe said. "Instead of a Doggy Dash, you can have a Doggy Splash!"

"Speaking of dogs," Frank asked as he looked around the room, "where's Stan?"

Joe's stomach did a triple flip when he saw no Stan and the door open. "Omigosh!" he gasped. "Stan escaped!"

"Is that him?" Mr. Frederick asked, pointing out the window. "The terrier rolling in the mud puddle?"

"Mud puddle?" Frank cried as he and Joe raced to the window. They glanced down and groaned. Stan had joined the mob of muddy mutts!

"Great," Frank muttered. "What are we going to tell Aunt Trudy?"

• • •

"Who knew washing a dog would be so much work?" Frank said later that day. He and Joe had just spent an hour hosing down Stan in the yard, then drying him with a blow-dryer.

"Yeah," Joe said with a frown. "Too bad we had to take Stan home before Dalmatian Lavation!"

Stan was now safe in Aunt Trudy's apartment, eating a hearty bowl of dog food. The boys were in the kitchen, getting plates and silverware to set the table for dinner.

Mr. Hardy was placing a pan of macaroni and cheese into the oven. Mrs. Hardy stood at the counter making a salad. They both knew what had happened at the Mud Bud Run and all about the brothers' new case.

"At least you guys got to rule out another suspect," Mr. Hardy said as he closed the oven door. "Any left?"

"Oliver Splathall," Joe said firmly. "He's got to be guilty."

"Because of his muddy boots?" Frank scoffed.

"Not just the boots, Frank," Joe said. "Oliver wanted to use the mud pit for his sculptures. When he couldn't, he said something about another plan!"

"But where would Oliver get all those frogs?" Frank asked.

"Fenton, didn't we meet the Splathalls on Parent-Teacher Night?" Mrs. Hardy asked as she tore lettuce. "They were sharing a website they built to show their son's sculptures."

"I remember the site was called Sculptures by Oliver," Mr. Hardy said. "That boy may have muddy boots, but he also has talent."

Joe stopped carrying dishes to the dining room when he heard about the website. "Hey, Frank," he said. "Maybe that website has more than Oliver's sculptures. Maybe it has clues."

"It's worth a try," Frank agreed. He turned to their parents and said, "Could we be excused for a few minutes to use the computer?"

"We'll set the table superfast after we get back," Joe promised. "Without breaking any plates."

"Okay, but no more than fifteen minutes," Mrs. Hardy said. "Dinner will be ready soon."

The brothers left the kitchen for the computer in the den. Joe searched for *Sculptures by Oliver* and the website appeared.

"Check it out," he said.

The home page showed a picture of Oliver in

a room, sculpting a skyscraper from hundreds of Popsicle sticks. There were other sculptures in the room made from recycled plastic bottles, paper clips—even egg cartons!

"It looks like Oliver's got a studio just for sculpting," said Joe.

Frank leaned forward in his chair to get a closer look. "It's not just for sculpting," he said. "Oliver uses it as a playroom, too."

Frank pointed to games and books in the picture, stacked on shelves and on the floor. But there was something next to the shelves that caught Joe's eye.

"What's that thing on the table?" he asked. "It looks like some kind of giant fish tank."

Frank enlarged the image until the tank was full screen. Instead of fish, the tank was filled with tiny swimming creatures with long tails.

"Those look like tadpoles," Frank said.

Tadpoles?

Joe stared at his brother. "I learned about tadpoles

in school," he said excitedly. "Do you know what they grow up to be? Well, do you?"

Frank's eyes widened as he remembered what he knew about tadpoles too.

"I sure do," he said slowly. "They grow up to be—frogs!"

Chapter

8

GROWING TADPOLES

"Do you think Oliver grew his own frogs?" Joe asked. "Then dumped them in the mud pit?"

"The tadpoles in that picture are nowhere near frogs yet," Frank pointed out. "How would Oliver have fully grown frogs to throw in the mud pit?"

"Unless the picture was taken while they were still tadpoles," Joe guessed. "Those taddies could have grown into froggies by now."

"True," Frank agreed.

"And who knows?" Joe went on. "Oliver could have saved some frogs as pets."

"Pet frogs?" exclaimed Frank.

"Kids have pet rats, iguanas, even pigs," Joe explained. "If we find frogs in Oliver's studio, we'll know he could have done it."

"I heard some tanks can hold up to twenty tadpoles," Frank said. "And twenty tadpoles become twenty frogs."

"More than that," said Joe, nodding at the screen. "Look at the size of Oliver's tank—it's huge!"

After Frank reduced the picture, they noticed something else. In the corner of the page was a schedule for Oliver's sculpture shows.

"Oliver is unveiling his new 'mud-sterpiece' tomorrow at noon," Frank noted. "Right in his backyard."

"I'll bet the mud he used was from the park," said Joe. "He could have dumped the frogs, then taken some mud, too."

"Oliver did say he liked the lumpy mud in the park," Frank remembered.

"And his boots were muddy!" Joe added. "I guess this means we're going to a mud sculpture show tomorrow."

"For sure," Frank said. "But while everyone else looks at Oliver's latest mud-sterpiece—we're going to look for frogs!"

"Whoa," Joe exclaimed. "Look at the turnout!"

It was the next day, and Frank and Joe were in the Splathalls' backyard for Oliver's sculpture show. It was still spring break, so most of the guests were kids.

In the middle of the yard was Oliver's mud-sterpiece, covered with a long white sheet until the big reveal later.

"So we've made it to Oliver's show," Joe whispered to Frank. "Now how do we get into his studio?"

"Let's ask Oliver or his parents," Frank said. "They don't have to know we'll be looking for clues."

The brothers looked around the yard. Oliver was busily talking to Dusty De Sancho, the ten-year-old reporter of the *Bayport Elementary School News*. Mrs.

Splathall was snapping pictures of the event with a professional camera. Mr. Splathall was in the yard too, carrying a tray of cookies among the guests.

The warm spring day felt more like summer, with dark rain clouds in the sky. But the chance of rain did not stop Oliver's fans from showing up for his mud-sterpiece.

"I can't wait to see Oliver's work," a girl was saying. "I'm sure it will be fabulous as always."

"My favorite was Oliver's snow sculpture of his foot," a boy declared. "The juxtaposition of the toes was no less than brilliant!"

The brothers walked around Oliver's sculpture. But while Joe was trying to guess what was underneath the sheet, Frank was busy noticing something else. . . .

"Look," he said, pointing out three holes in the ground. "It looks like a three-legged camera stand was right here by the sculpture."

"Mrs. Splathall probably took pictures of Oliver's sculpture," Joe decided, "so she can post it on his website after the big reveal."

"Hey, Frank, Joe!" a familiar voice called.

The brothers turned and were surprised to see Chet walking over.

"What are you doing here, Chet?" asked Joe.

"I didn't know you were an art fan," Frank said.

"I'm not really," Chet said. "But I am a fan of cookies and fruit punch."

He pointed to a punch bowl on a nearby table. There, filling a paper cup, was a man wearing overalls and a big smile. The brothers recognized him at once.

"Frank, isn't that guy Blurpy Bob?" Joe asked, "From the frog farm?"

"Yeah, but what's he doing here?" Frank wondered.

Using his free hand, Blurpy Bob grabbed a cookie from Mr. Splathall's tray. Mr. Splathall turned away from Bob, then headed toward Frank, Joe, and Chet.

"How about a snack, guys?" Mr. Splathall asked. "I hope you like mud cookies!"

"Thanks!" Chet said, taking one.

Frank and Joe stared at the tray.

"Did you say . . . *mud* cookies, Mr. Splathall?" Joe asked.

"Um . . . are they made of mud?" Frank added.

"Just chocolate and marshmallows, guys," Mr. Splathall chuckled. "So dig in!"

"Actually," Frank blurted, "we'd rather see Oliver's studio before the big reveal."

"If Oliver is busy, we can look around ourselves," added Joe.

"That's a good idea," Mr. Splathall said. He pointed at the side of the house. "Go through the green door and down the stairs to the basement. That's where Oliver's studio is."

"Thanks, Mr. Splathall!" said Frank.

As Oliver's father carried his tray to another group of kids, Chet said, "What was that all about?"

"We're looking for frogs," Joe said. "Want to help?"

Chet stared at Joe. "Frogs?"

"A ton of frogs were found in the mud run yesterday," Joe said. "So we're checking out Oliver Splathall's tadpole tank."

"I'll pass," Chet decided. "I'd rather check out the brownies next to the punch!"

Frank and Joe wasted no time finding Oliver's studio. The room looked just like it did on the website, except for one thing: the Popsicle-stick sculpture had been replaced by a huge globby pink one!

"Whoa, Frank," Joe said, studying the sculpture.

"It looks like a pink gnome with huge, flat feet!"

"It smells familiar too," said Frank, taking a whiff. "Like bubblegum."

"Awesome!" Joe exclaimed. "Oliver made a whole sculpture from chewed-up bubblegum wads!"

Joe reached out to touch it, but Frank grabbed his arm. "Bubblegum is sticky!" he said. "Let's check out the tadpole tank."

The big tadpole tank was still on the same table. When the boys peered through the glass, they saw a slew of tiny frogs swimming in the water.

"The tadpoles did grow into frogs," Joe pointed out.

"Not totally yet," said Frank. "They're way smaller than the ones in the mud pit."

He noticed a tablet on the table. Paused on the screen was a video of Oliver sculpting in his backyard.

"That's probably what the three-legged camera stand was for," Frank said. "Check it out, Joe . . . Joe?"

"Um . . . over here," Joe's voice quavered.

Frank turned and gasped. Joe was standing on

the foot of the bubblegum gnome. His own foot had sunk all the way down into the gum!

"Joe, will you get off?" Frank said. "I told you not to touch it."

"I didn't touch it, I stepped in it," Joe groaned. "And now I'm stuck. . . . Help!"

Chapter
9

SCULPTURE STANDOFF

Frank raced across the room to the bubblegum sculpture. He tried to yank Joe's foot out of the gum, but it was jammed in too tight!

"I don't want to be stuck here forever!" Joe wailed. "Step on it, Frank!"

"You're the one who stepped on it," Frank muttered. He leaned in for a better grip—only to get his hair stuck on the gnome's bubblegum arm!

"What's happened, Frank?" Joe asked.

"Now I'm stuck!" Frank exclaimed. "Why can't Oliver just chew gum like the rest of us?"

"Because I'm an artist, that's why," a voice replied.

Frank and Joe turned the best they could to see Oliver.

"My dad told me you were down here," Oliver said. "How come?"

Joe thought fast. "Because we're really attached to your work?" he blurted.

"Yeah, I can see that," Oliver said with a frown. "Luckily, I've got a spray to get you guys unstuck."

He grabbed a can of Good-bye Goo from a shelf and sprayed the gnome's foot and arm. After a few seconds, Frank and Joe were free.

"Thanks, Oliver," Frank said.

"No problem," Oliver said, placing the can back on the shelf. "Bubblegum can be a tad sticky."

"Tad?" Joe declared. He swung around to point to the tank. "As in . . . tadpoles?"

Oliver raised an eyebrow and asked, "What about them?"

"Tons of frogs were found in the park mud pit

yesterday," Frank explained. "We wanted to find out if they were yours."

"I heard about the frogs at the mud run," Oliver said, nodding. "But they weren't mine."

He nodded toward the tank. "As you can see," he said, "my frogs are still froglets—small frogs, not fully grown."

"Unless you ordered fully grown frogs from Blurpy Bob's," Joe suggested, "so you could throw them in the mud run yesterday."

"Blurpy Bob is here today," Frank pointed out, "so he must know you."

"What's the matter, Ollie?" said Joe, folding his arms across his chest. "Forget your complimentary frog chow?"

"First of all, I told you I hate the name Ollie!" Oliver insisted. "Second of all, do you really think I put those frogs in the mud pit?"

"It depends," Frank said. "Where were you early yesterday morning from about seven to ten?"

"That's easy," Oliver said with a smile. "I was working on my latest mud-sterpiece."

"The one out in the yard?" Joe asked.

Oliver nodded and said, "I wanted to get an early start so it would be dry by today."

"So the video on the tablet is of you making that sculpture?" Frank asked.

"You bet," Oliver agreed. He picked up the device and held it out to the brothers. "Play it and see for yourselves."

Frank took the tablet and pressed the arrow on the screen. The video began showing Oliver sculpting a big pile of mud. But that wasn't all the Hardys noticed.

"The video has the time and date in the corner," Frank told Joe. "It was shot yesterday morning at seven ten."

"It also shows how long the video is," Joe said. "It's three whole hours!"

"Three hours of total genius!" Oliver declared. "I started at around seven and ended at ten."

Joe tugged Frank a few feet away from Oliver. "If Oliver was sculpting yesterday morning," he whispered, "he couldn't have been in the park."

"So he couldn't have dumped those frogs in the mud pit," Frank whispered back.

Oliver's mom suddenly called down from the top of the stairs, "Oliver, please unveil your sculpture before it rains. The sky is getting darker and darker by the minute!"

"Coming, Mom!" Oliver called back.

As the boys headed upstairs, Joe said, "I thought you had no mud to make your sculpture, Oliver."

"That's what I thought," Oliver said with a grin. "So was I surprised when I came across a whole mud pit in my backyard."

"How'd you miss a mud pit in your own back-yard?" Joe asked.

Oliver just shrugged. "I don't know, guess I've been kind of wrapped up in this project."

"Makes sense," Frank said as they all walked out-side. "Sometimes we can only focus on the mystery we're trying to solve."

Oliver nodded and headed over to his mud sculp-ture. Frank and Joe walked toward the crowd.

Joe sighed. "With Oliver innocent, we have no more suspects. Zero . . . zilch . . . zip."

Before joining the others, the brothers checked out one last thing: a shallow pit at the end of the backyard filled with mud!

"Oliver wasn't lying about mud in his backyard," Joe concluded. "There's plenty here for ten whole sculptures."

"That's for sure," Frank agreed. "Now let's go see what Oliver made with all that mud."

He and Joe joined Chet at the covered sculpture. By now all the guests had gathered for the big reveal.

"All this fuss for a mud pie," Chet whispered. "Give me a break."

Soon all eyes were on Oliver as began his speech:

"Thank you all for celebrating the reveal of my latest mud-sterpiece. To me a new creation can only represent—"

"Oliver," Mrs. Splathall interrupted. "The rain!"

"We need speed, son," Mr. Splathall called. "Not accuracy."

Oliver glanced up at the darkening sky. "Oh

yeah," he said. "So without further ado, may I proudly introduce—*A Breath of Spring*!"

Mrs. Splathall pointed her camera at Oliver as he gave the sheet a yank. It fluttered to the ground to a chorus of oohs and aahs!

"Fabulous!" Dusty swooned as she scribbled on her reporter's pad.

"It's the embodiment of antiquity," a boy declared, "in the modern age!"

Chet turned to Frank and Joe. "It's a nose!" he said. "A giant muddy nose!"

Frank, Joe, and Chet stared at the mud sculpture, a few inches taller than Oliver. It was a sculpture of a nose with giant flaring nostrils.

"That's awesome, Oliver!" Frank shouted.

"Seriously," Joe said. "That's one impressive mud pie."

The boys made their way through the yard to get a better look but stopped in their tracks when they heard a weird, familiar noise.

"Chet? Did you just croak like a frog to be funny?" Frank asked.

"No," Chet said. "Why?"

Frank shook his head and said, "It's just that I thought I heard—"

"Frogs!" Joe cut in. "I hear them too—listen!"

The boys stopped to hear a croak. Then a blurp. Then a whole chorus of croaks and blurps coming faster and louder!

"It sounds like frogs!" Joe exclaimed.

"Where are they?" asked Frank, looking around.

"There!" Chet shouted.

Frank and Joe looked to see where Chet was pointing. Popping out of Oliver's nose sculpture one by one were . . . frogs!

Guests screamed and shrieked as the frogs from the nose landed on the ground, hopping over feet and between legs. The only ones smiling were Blurpy Bob and Dusty De Sancho. . . .

"What a scoop!" Dusty cheered as she wrote in her reporter's pad. "This story is better than the skunk in the school cafeteria!"

"Oliver!" Mrs. Splathall cried as she brushed a

frog off her sneaker with her camera. "Is this some kind of joke?"

"I didn't put frogs in my sculpture, Mom!" Oliver insisted. "I don't have a clue how they got there!"

Joe couldn't believe what he was seeing. Where had all the frogs come from?

"Oliver's not the only who doesn't have a clue," he told Frank. "Neither do I!"

THE HARDY BOYS—and
YOU!

READY TO JOIN FRANK AND JOE IN CRACKING THE CASE

of the croaker confusion? Grab a piece of paper and write your answers down. Or turn the page to find out!

1. Frank and Joe ruled out the Zamora kids, Mr. Frederick, and Oliver Splathall as suspects. Who else might have put all the frogs in the mud?

2. Can you think of other ways frogs might have gotten into the mud pit and Oliver's sculpture?

3. When starting a mystery, Frank and Joe ask themselves *who*, *what*, *where*, *when*, and *why*. Can you come up with more words a detective might ask himself or herself?

4. Which clues helped you to solve this mystery?

Chapter 10

SPRING BREAK RETAKE

The frogs hopped out of control, all over the Splathalls' yard. The only one who didn't seem to mind was Chet.

"As long as they don't jump in the punch bowl," Chet said. "I'm going for seconds."

He gave a little wave, then headed for the snack table. But the only thing Frank and Joe were hungry for were answers!

"How did frogs get into Oliver's sculpture?" Joe wondered.

The brothers' thoughts were interrupted by Mr. Splathall shouting, "Look!"

Frank and Joe looked to see where Mr. Splathall was pointing. Popping out of the mud pit in the Splathalls' yard were frogs. Dozens of them!

"That's where Oliver got the mud for his sculpture!" said Frank.

"First the Mud Bud Run, then Oliver's sculpture, and now that mud pit too?" Joe cried. "Nobody would have that many frogs to go around!"

Nobody?

Frank repeated the word under his breath. Then his eyes lit up with an idea. "What if nobody put the frogs in those places?" he asked.

"What do you mean?" said Joe.

"What if the frogs are supposed to be in the mud," Frank explained, "because they're frogs?"

He noticed Joe's puzzled face. "Come on, Joe," he said, "let's ask an expert."

The brothers walked over to Blurpy Bob. After they introduced themselves, Frank said, "What do you know about those frogs, Bob?"

"I know they're coming out of hibernation," Bob said with a grin, "after a long, cold winter."

"Hibernation?" Frank repeated. "You mean frogs sleep in the mud?"

"Not exactly sleep," Bob explained. "Some frogs burrow in the mud, then gently freeze until the first warm days of spring. That's when they thaw almost all at once!"

"Frogs in the park mud pit never happened before," Frank said. "Why this spring?"

Bob shrugged. "Frogs pick different places to hibernate," he said. "I guess critters like to mix it up too."

"Wow!" Joe exclaimed. He turned to Frank and smiled. So that explained the frogs in the mud. But it still didn't explain something else. . . .

"What are you doing at Oliver's mud sculpture show, Bob?" Joe asked. "Did you know the frogs would be getting their spring wake-up call?"

Bob laughed as he shook his head. "I sold Oliver his tadpole tank, so his mom invited me to his next sculpture show."

"You mean his last," Joe sighed.

He pointed to Oliver jumping up and down, shouting, "I'm done with mud sculptures! From now on I'm sticking with bubblegum! And Popsicle sticks! And toe jam!"

"Toe jam?" Frank whispered.

"He can't be serious," answered Joe.

Blurpy Bob turned to Frank and Joe and said,

"Nice meeting you, guys. Now I'd better catch a few frogs!"

Bob got to work and so did Joe. He pulled out his clue book. Then he wrote:

Who did it: Nature!
Why: Because frozen frogsicles survive the winter!

"Too bad the frogs' timing was bad," Frank said. "For Oliver's mud sculpture show and the Mud Bud Run yesterday."

The brothers glanced up as the first drops of rain trickled down. Seconds later the clouds seemed to burst as rain gushed from the sky.

"The frogs might have had bad timing, Frank," Joe shouted as they raced into Oliver's house, "but I think this rain is right on time!"

The spring rain sprang a huge surprise. It rained for two whole days, leaving plenty of thick, fresh mud for a new Mud Bud Run later that week. This one would be right behind Bayport Elementary School!

All the kids from the last mud run were there, T-shirts still clean and new. Frank and Joe were right at the front.

"Thanks to all that rain," Frank told Joe, "the Mud Bud Run is getting a second chance."

"Yeah," Joe agreed. "I just hope this one is frog free."

Frank turned to Joe. "You remember what Blurpy Bob told us?" he asked. "Frogs hibernate in the winter, not the spring."

"Yeah, and I think I know why!" Joe said.

"Why?" asked Frank.

"Because spring is too much fun!" Joe replied to the sound of Coach Lambert's whistle. "Come on, Frank—let's get muddy!"

FOLLOW THE TRAIL AND SOLVE MYSTERIES WITH FRANK AND JOE!

HardyBoysSeries.com

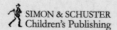